This book is dedicated to all the great readers at New Hampton Community School in New Hampton, New Hampshire.

This book is also dedicated to my 4th grade teacher, Mrs. Beattie, who never gave up on me and brought the joy of reading into my life.

Thank you to my husband, Roger, and our two children, Audrey and Ben, who inspire me every day.

For my Aunt Dot, who was always there with an encouraging word and positive thought.

Last but not least, this book is dedicated to my life coach, Emily Clement, who showed me how to reinvent myself from the inside out.

www.mascotbooks.com

Stanley Big Thumbs

For more information, please contact:
Mascot Books
620 Herndon Parkway, Suite 320
Herndon, VA 20170
info@mascotbooks.com

Library of Congress Control Number: 2018906352

CPSIA Code: PBANG0918A
ISBN-13: 978-1-68401-974-8

Printed in the United States

Stanley Big Thumbs

Dorothy Prive'

illustrated by Amber Chunko

Stanley the cat was born on a warm, spring day in a barn's hayloft.

Stanley was a happy kitten. He grew quickly, just like his brothers and sisters, except for his thumbs which were already huge.

When Stanley was learning to hunt mice, he would sometimes trip over his own paws because his thumbs stuck out.

Some of the other animals that lived on the farm thought it was funny and would laugh at him every time it happened.

One day, Stanley's mom, Pretty, took him aside and said, "Don't pay those animals any mind. They don't know how special you are!

You've been given a special gift with those thumbs, even if it doesn't always seem like it. Try to find a way to make your big thumbs work for you instead of against you."

As time went by, Stanley grew into those big paws of his. He remembered what his mom said and learned to use his thumbs to become one of the best hunters on the farm! The mice didn't stand a chance! The farmer and his wife were very happy that Stanley lived on their farm!

Stanley became a good climber, too! He used his extra big thumbs to climb quickly up trees. When a fox came around looking to catch something to feed her young, she could never catch Stanley!

One day, while Stanley was hunting mice around
the farmer's house, he smelled something
unusual. Then he saw it. It was smoke!

Stanley was smart and knew this billowing gray stuff didn't smell right. He decided to run and look for the farmer to make sure he was okay.

Stanley clawed up the
pole to the hayloft, but the
farmer wasn't there.

Stanley looked and looked. Soon, the sun began to come up. It was early in the morning. Stanley kept searching everywhere for the farmer. He even ran through the cow barn!

Then he realized the farmer was in the house. Stanley quickly ran back and climbed up a tree branch close to an open window and leaped inside.

Once inside, all Stanley could see was smoke. He didn't know where he was, so he ran all over the house looking for the farmer. Finally, he saw the farmer and his wife sleeping in bed.

Stanley was scared of the smoke but happy to find the farmer. He quickly jumped on the farmer and dug those big thumbs of his into the farmer's chest to wake him up.

The farmer shouted out, surprised, and sat straight up as Stanley jumped off the side of the bed. The farmer smelled the smoke and hollered, "FIRE!"

His wife was up in an instant and they both quickly made their way downstairs.

The smoke was pouring from the kitchen! The farmer ran in and saw that the smoke was coming from the stove. It was a chimney fire!

The farmer quickly ran to the phone and dialed 911, telling the operator what he'd woken up to. The firemen knew where the farmer lived, so they hurried over.

The fire department arrived at the farm with their big, red firetruck—its siren blaring! They were quickly able to put the fire in the chimney out.

After the firemen told the farmer that it was okay to go back inside the house, the farmer and his wife went in to look at the damage.

The firemen told them that they were very lucky they called when they did because they could have lost the whole house, not just the chimney.

"How did you know there was a fire?" one of the firemen asked. "It looks like your smoke detector didn't go off."

That's when the farmer remembered Stanley jumping on him. "Can you help me find that black cat named Stanley?" he asked his wife. "We owe him a big thank you!"

The farmer and his wife thanked the fireman before they headed outside to look for Stanley. They couldn't see him outside, so they started calling his name.

"Stanley! Here kitty, kitty! Staaannnllley!"

It turned out that Stanley was hiding in a bale of hay, so the farmer and his wife suspected that he would need some coaxing out. They ran to the house and got a saucer of milk.

When they set it down in the barn, Stanley saw that milk shimmering in the bowl and couldn't resist. He ran right out for it! Milk was his favorite.

From that day on, the farmer and his wife were so grateful that they insisted Stanley never sleep in the barn again. Instead, he had a nice, cozy bed right in front of the fire. He also got a saucer of milk every night.

Stanley still hunted mice for the farmer and his wife, but he was always welcome in the house. Now he was part of the family!

About the Author

Dorothy "Dolly" Prive' lives in Bristol, New Hampshire, with her wonderful husband of 32 years. She has two great kids; one grandson, Killian; and one granddaughter, Amora.